by Cathy Vonderau

illustrated by Felix Eddy

Printed in the United States of America.

ISBN: 978-1-63385-152-8

Library of Congress Control Number: 2016909873

Illustrated by Felix Eddy

Designed and published by

Word Association Publishers
205 Fifth Avenue
Tarentum, Pennsylvania 15084

www.wordassociation.com
1.800.827.7903

For Dean, Darren and Doria

Acknowledgments

Thank you to Robert for his invaluable help as a Beta Reader, and for giving me ideas for illustrations. I hope we can work together in the future. It was a pleasure.

My friends at the Critique Group North had suggestions which were encouraging, and I thank them, especially MaryAlice Meli and Jon Saari.

Felix Eddy, my illustrator was great to work with. Let's do it again.

BREAD

Mother **LOVED** her big red purse.

Grandma gave it to her before she left.
Mother was always looking for something
in the big red purse.

One morning, Mother sat the big red purse on the kitchen table. She pulled out a comb, a wallet, a tissue, a cell phone, a pocket calendar, and a chocolate bar.

"Where is it?"

BREAD
DAILY PLANNER

Mother was annoyed. She stuffed the cell phone in her jeans' pocket and ate the chocolate bar.

"Sissy," Grandpa laughed. "you remind me of your mother. She was always digging in that purse. What are you looking for?"

"I'm looking for the instructions for this big red purse."

"You need instructions?" Grandpa asked. "Just put your things in it. But be careful. One of these days, you're going to fall into that big red purse."

Mother reached **deeper** into the big red purse.

Her arm went in up to her shoulder. She pulled out a pink piggy bank, a pair of zebra slippers, and six fruit juice boxes. She yanked out a lava lamp, an easy chair and a bookcase.

Still **NO** instructions but Mother was determined.

BREAD
APPLE
APPLE
APPLE
JUICE

BREAD
APPLE
APPLE
APPLE
JUICE
JUICE

As I quietly sipped my juice box, to my surprise, Mother suddenly climbed up on the kitchen chair, leaned way over the big red purse-and dived in.

"MOTHER... are you okay?" I called.

My voice made an echo. Shouting down a purse seemed silly, but my Mother was down there!

After a few anxious seconds, my cell phone rang.

"Of course I'm okay, Chuck. I need you to go to the garage and bring back the longest piece of rope you can find.
I'll hold."

"Got it, Mother!" I said running back from the garage.

Next she told me to hold onto one end of the rope and send the rest down the purse.

BREAD
APPLE
APPLE
APPLE
APPLE
APPLE
APPLE
DAILY PLANNER

"Now take the big red purse out to the driveway and tell Grandpa to attach your end of the rope to the bumper of his old car. Tell him to drive very slowly down the driveway."

By the time Grandpa got to the end of the driveway, Mother popped her head out of the big red purse.

"Chuck," said Mother, "hurry, grab Grandma!"

"GRANDMA!" Grandpa shouted as he ran up the driveway, not knowing whether to laugh or cry. "I thought you ran away."

"Edward, I would never leave you. I just fell into the big red purse and couldn't get out. Thank goodness Sissy found my note."

10

BREAD

I thought Mother would throw away that big red purse. It caused so much trouble. But Mother said no. She said it was a good place to be when you need peace and quiet. Just tie a rope on Grandpa's bumper before you go.

About the Author

Cathy Vonderau has loved to read and write since she was a little girl. Her favorite stories were fairy tales and mysteries, and still are. Cathy is from Pittsburgh PA. There are lots of good fairy tales and mysteries there, so she'll probably stay.

HOT CHOCOLATE
BOOKS